# The Best Book of
# NURSERY
# RHYMES

### Illustrated by Carolyn Dinan

Rock-a-bye, baby,
Thy cradle is green,
Father's a nobleman,
Mother's a queen;

And Betty's a lady,
And wears a gold ring;
And Johnny's a drummer,
And drums for the king.

Round and round the garden
Like a teddy bear;

One step, two step,
Tickle you under there!

This little pig went to market,
This little pig stayed at home,

This little pig had roast beef,
This little pig had none,

And this little pig cried, Wee-wee-wee-wee-wee,
I can't find my way home!

Pat-a-cake, pat-a-cake, baker's man,
Bake me a cake as fast as you can;
Pat it and prick it, and mark it with B,
Put it in the oven for baby and me.

Dance to your daddy,
My little babby,
Dance to your daddy, my little lamb.
You shall have a fishy
In a little dishy,
You shall have a fishy when the boat comes in.

Wee Willie Winkie runs through the town,
Upstairs and downstairs in his nightgown,
Rapping at the window, crying through the lock,
Are the children all in bed? It's past eight o'clock.

Little Bo-peep has lost her sheep,
And can't tell where to find them;
Leave them alone, and they'll come home,
And bring their tails behind them.

Little Bo-peep fell fast asleep,
And dreamt she heard them bleating;
But when she awoke, she found it a joke,
For they were still all fleeting.

Then up she took her little crook,
Determined for to find them;
She found them indeed, but it made her heart bleed,
For they'd left their tails behind them.

It happened one day, as Bo-peep did stray
Into a meadow hard by,
There she espied their tails side by side,
All hung on a tree to dry.

She heaved a sigh, and wiped her eye,
And over the hillocks went rambling,
And tried what she could, as a shepherdess should,
To tack again each to its lambkin.

Oh where, oh where has my little dog gone?
Oh where, oh where can he be?
With his ears cut short and his tail cut long,
Oh where, oh where is he?

There was a crooked man, and he walked a crooked mile,
He found a crooked sixpence against a crooked stile:
He bought a crooked cat, which caught a crooked mouse,
And they all lived together in a little crooked house.

Little Miss Muffet
Sat on a tuffet,
Eating her curds and whey;

There came a big spider,
Who sat down beside her
And frightened Miss Muffet away.

Two little dicky birds,
Sitting on a wall;
One named Peter,
The other named Paul.
Fly away, Peter!
Fly away, Paul!
Come back, Peter!
Come back, Paul!

Georgie Porgie, pudding and pie,
Kissed the girls and made them cry;
When the boys came out to play,
Georgie Porgie ran away.

Pussy cat, pussy cat, where have you been?
I've been to London to look at the queen.
Pussy cat, pussy cat, what did you there?
I frightened a little mouse under her chair.

One, two,
Buckle my shoe;
Three, four,
Knock at the door;
Five, six,
Pick up sticks;
Seven, eight,
Lay them straight;
Nine, ten,
A big fat hen;
Eleven, twelve,
Dig and delve;
Thirteen, fourteen,
Maids a-courting;
Fifteen, sixteen,
Maids in the kitchen;
Seventeen, eighteen,
Maids in waiting;
Nineteen, twenty,
My plate's empty.

Hickory, dickory, dock,
The mouse ran up the clock.
The clock struck one,
The mouse ran down,
Hickory, dickory, dock.

Three blind mice, see how they run!
They all ran after the farmer's wife,
Who cut off their tails with a carving knife,
Did you ever see such a thing in your life,
As three blind mice?

Rub-a-dub-dub,
Three men in a tub,
And who do you think they be?
The butcher, the baker,
The candlestick-maker,
And they all sailed out to sea.

Old King Cole
Was a merry old soul,
And a merry old soul was he;
He called for his pipe,
And he called for his bowl,
And he called for his fiddlers three.

Every fiddler, he had a fiddle,
And a very fine fiddle had he;
Twee tweedle dee, tweedle dee, went the fiddlers.
Oh, there's none so rare
As can compare
With King Cole and his fiddlers three.

Ding dong bell,
Pussy's in the well.
Who put her in?
Little Johnny Green.
Who pulled her out?
Little Tommy Stout.
What a naughty boy was that,
To try to drown poor pussy cat,
Who never did any harm,
And killed the mice in his father's barn.

Jack and Jill went up the hill
To fetch a pail of water;
Jack fell down and broke his crown,
And Jill came tumbling after.

Up Jack got, and home did trot,
As fast as he could caper,
To old Dame Dob, who patched his nob
With vinegar and brown paper.

Then Jill came in,
And she did grin,
To see Jack's paper plaster;
Her mother whipped her,
Across her knee,
For laughing at Jack's disaster.

A was an archer, who shot at a frog,
B was a butcher, and had a great dog.
C was a captain, all covered with lace,
D was a drunkard, and had a red face.
E was an esquire, with pride on his brow,
F was a farmer, and followed the plough.
G was a gamester, who had but ill-luck,
H was a hunter and hunted a buck.
I was an innkeeper, who loved to carouse,
J was a joiner, and built up a house.
K was King William, once governed this land,
L was a lady, who had a white hand.
M was a miser, and hoarded up gold,

N was a nobleman, gallant and bold.
O was an oyster girl, and went about town,
P was a parson, and wore a black gown.
Q was a queen, who wore a silk slip,
R was a robber, and wanted a whip.
S was a sailor, and spent all he got,
T was a tinker, and mended a pot.
U was a usurer, a miserable elf,
V was a vintner, who drank all himself.
W was a watchman, and guarded the door,
X was expensive, and so became poor.
Y was a youth, that did not love school,
Z was a zany, a poor harmless fool.

Simple Simon met a pieman,
Going to the fair;
Says Simple Simon to the pieman,
Let me taste your ware.

Says the pieman to Simple Simon,
Show me first your penny;
Says Simple Simon to the pieman,
Indeed I have not any.

Simple Simon went a-fishing,
For to catch a whale;
All the water he had got
Was in his mother's pail.

Simple Simon went to look
If plums grew on a thistle;
He pricked his finger very much,
Which made poor Simon whistle.

Sing a song of sixpence,
A pocket full of rye;
Four and twenty blackbirds,
Baked in a pie.

When the pie was opened,
The birds began to sing;
Was not that a dainty dish,
To set before the king?

The king was in his counting-house,
Counting out his money;
The queen was in the parlour,
Eating bread and honey.

The maid was in the garden,
Hanging out the clothes,
There came a little blackbird,
And snapped off her nose.

If all the world were paper,
And all the sea were ink,
If all the trees were bread and cheese,
What should we have to drink?

The Queen of Hearts
She made some tarts,
All on a summer's day;
The Knave of Hearts
He stole the tarts,
And took them clean away.

The King of Hearts
Called for the tarts,
And beat the knave full sore;
The Knave of Hearts
Brought back the tarts,
And vowed he'd steal no more.

Hark, hark, the dogs do bark,
Beggars are coming to town,
Some in tatters and some in rags,
And some in velvet gowns.

Some gave them white bread,
And some gave them brown,
And some gave them a good horse-whip,
And sent them out of town.

Humpty Dumpty sat on a wall,
Humpty Dumpty had a great fall.
All the king's horses,
And all the king's men,
Couldn't put Humpty together again.

There was an old woman who lived in a shoe,
She had so many children she didn't know what to do!
She gave them some broth without any bread,
She whipped them all soundly and put them to bed.

I had a little nut tree,
Nothing would it bear
But a silver nutmeg
And a golden pear;

The King of Spain's daughter
Came to visit me,
And all for the sake
Of my little nut tree.

Moses supposes his toeses are roses,
But Moses supposes erroneously;
For nobody's toeses are posies of roses
As Moses supposes his toeses to be.

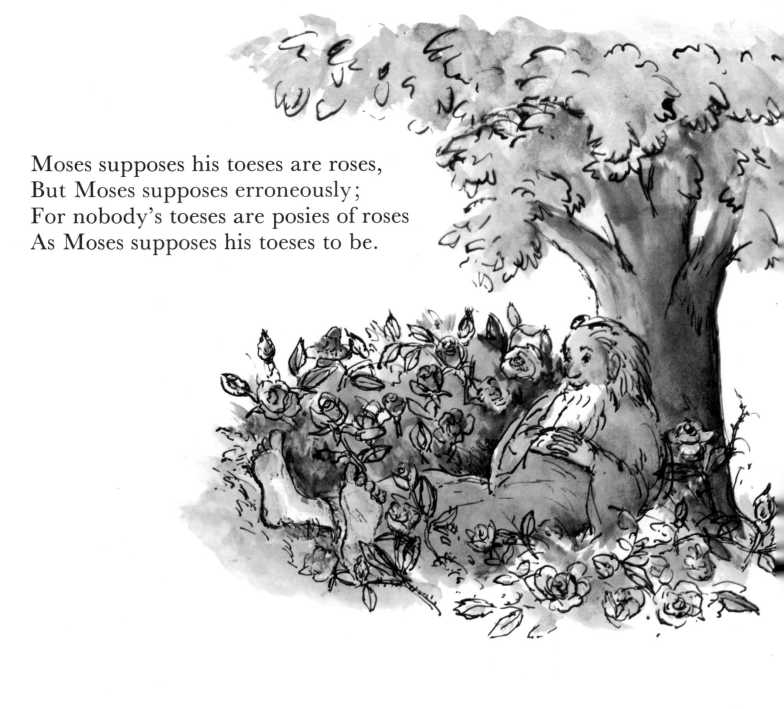

Little Polly Flinders
Sat among the cinders,
Warming her pretty little toes;
Her mother came and caught her,
And whipped her little daughter
For spoiling her nice new clothes.

Elsie Marley grown so fine,
Won't get up to feed the swine.
Stays in bed till half past nine,
Lazy Elsie Marley!

Polly put the kettle on,
Polly put the kettle on,
Polly put the kettle on,
We'll all have tea.

Sukey take it off again,
Sukey take it off again,
Sukey take it off again,
They've all gone away.

This is the farmer sowing his corn,
That kept the cock that crowed in the morn,
That waked the priest all shaven and shorn,
That married the man all tattered and torn,
That kissed the maiden all forlorn,
That milked the cow with the crumpled horn,
That tossed the dog,
That worried the cat,
That killed the rat,
That ate the malt
That lay in the house that Jack built.

Lavender's blue, diddle, diddle,
Lavender's green;
When I am king, diddle, diddle,
You shall be queen.

Call up your men, diddle, diddle,
Set them to work,
Some to the plough, diddle, diddle,
Some to the cart.

Some to make hay, diddle, diddle,
Some to thresh corn,
Whilst you and I, diddle, diddle,
Keep ourselves warm.

Hey diddle diddle,
The cat and the fiddle,
The cow jumped over the moon;
The little dog laughed
To see such sport,
And the dish ran away with the spoon.

Boys and girls come out to play,
The moon doth shine as bright as day,
Leave your supper and leave your sleep,
And join your playfellows in the street.
Come with a whoop and come with a call,
Come with a good will or not at all.
Up the ladder and down the wall,
A half-penny loaf will serve us all;
You find milk and I'll find flour,
And we'll have a pudding in half an hour.

Oranges and lemons,
Say the bells of St. Clement's.

You owe me five farthings,
Say the bells of St. Martin's.

When will you pay me?
Say the bells of Old Bailey.

When I grow rich,
Say the bells of Shoreditch.

When will that be?
Say the bells of Stepney.

I'm sure I don't know,
Says the great bell at Bow.

Here comes a candle to light you to bed,
Here comes a chopper to chop off your head!

Thirty days hath September,
April, June and November;
All the rest have thirty-one,
Excepting February alone,
And that has twenty-eight days clear
And twenty-nine in each leap year.

Where are you going to, my pretty maid?
I'm going a-milking sir, she said,
Sir, she said, sir, she said,
I'm going a-milking, sir, she said.

May I go with you, my pretty maid?
You're kindly welcome, sir, she said.

Say, will you marry me, my pretty maid?
Yes, if you please, kind sir, she said.

What is your father, my pretty maid?
My father's a farmer, sir, she said.

What is your fortune, my pretty maid?
My face is my fortune, sir, she said.

Then I can't marry you, my pretty maid.
Nobody asked you, sir, she said.

Doctor Foster went to Gloucester
In a shower of rain:
He stepped in a puddle,
Right up to his middle,
And never went there again.

Jack Sprat could eat no fat,
His wife could eat no lean,
And so between them both, you see,
They licked the platter clean.

Bobby Shafto's gone to sea,
Silver buckles at his knee:
He'll come back and marry me,
Bonny Bobby Shafto!

Bobby Shafto's fat and fair,
Combing down his yellow hair;
He's my love for evermore,
Bonny Bobby Shafto!

Solomon Grundy,

Born on a Monday,

Christened on Tuesday,

Married on Wednesday,

Took ill on Thursday,

Worse on Friday,

Died on Saturday,

Buried on Sunday.

This is the end
Of Solomon Grundy.

Tom, Tom the piper's son,
Stole a pig and away he ran;
The pig was eat
And Tom was beat,
And Tom went howling down the street.

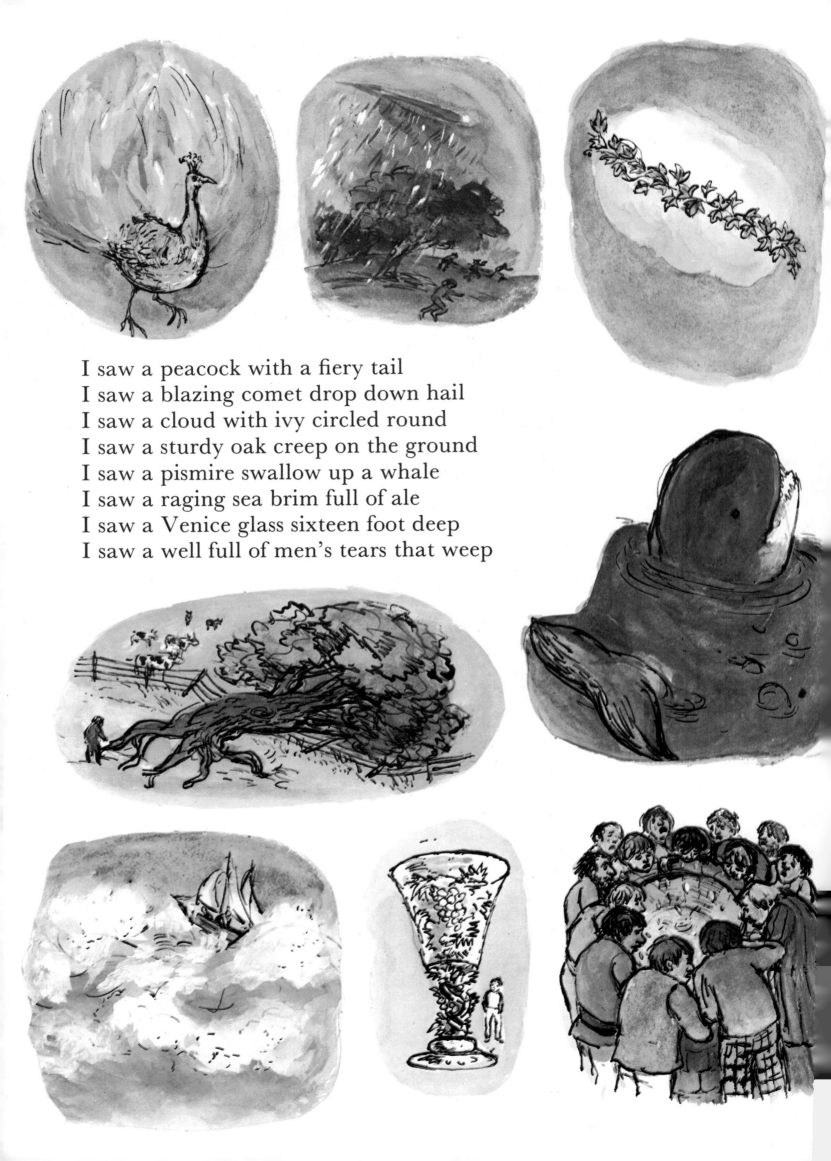

I saw a peacock with a fiery tail
I saw a blazing comet drop down hail
I saw a cloud with ivy circled round
I saw a sturdy oak creep on the ground
I saw a pismire swallow up a whale
I saw a raging sea brim full of ale
I saw a Venice glass sixteen foot deep
I saw a well full of men's tears that weep

I saw their eyes all in a flame of fire
I saw a house as big as the moon and higher
I saw the sun even in the midst of night
I saw the man that saw this wondrous sight.

I had a little pony,
His name was Dapple Gray;
I lent him to a lady
To ride a mile away.
She whipped him, she slashed him,
She rode him through the mire;
I would not lend my pony now,
For all the lady's hire.

The north wind doth blow,
And we shall have snow,
And what will poor robin do then?
Poor thing.
He'll sit in a barn,
And keep himself warm,
And hide his head under his wing.
Poor thing.

Old Mother Hubbard
Went to the cupboard,
To fetch her poor dog a bone;
But when she came there
The cupboard was bare
And so the poor dog had none.

She went to the baker's
To buy him some bread;
But when she came back
The poor dog was dead.

She went to the undertaker's
To buy him a coffin;
But when she came back
The poor dog was laughing.

She took a clean dish
To get him some tripe;
But when she came back
He was smoking a pipe.

She went to the hosier's
To buy him some hose;
But when she came back
He was dressed in his clothes.

The dame made a curtsey,
The dog made a bow;
The dame said, Your servant,
The dog said, Bow-wow.

Can you make me a cambric shirt,
Parsley, sage, rosemary and thyme,
Without any seam or needlework?
And you shall be a true lover of mine.

Can you wash it in yonder well,
Parsley, sage, rosemary and thyme,
Where never sprung water, nor rain ever fell?
And you shall be a true lover of mine.

Can you dry it on yonder thorn,
Parsley, sage, rosemary and thyme,
Which never bore blossom since Adam was born?
And you shall be a true lover of mine.

Monday's child is fair of face,
Tuesday's child is full of grace,
Wednesday's child is full of woe,
Thursday's child has far to go,
Friday's child is loving and giving,
Saturday's child works hard for his living,
And the child that is born on the Sabbath day
Is bonny and blithe, and good and gay.

Little Boy Blue,
Come blow your horn,
The sheep in the meadow,
The cow's in the corn;
But where is the boy
Who looks after the sheep?
He's under a haycock,
Fast asleep.